What's in the Truck?

Philip Ardagh · Jason Chapman

For Martin, Lord Roxbee, who's always loved cars.
P.A.

For Rodney and C.R.W.
who stopped my wheels falling off.
J.C.

First published in the UK in 2020
First published in the US in 2020
by Faber and Faber Limited
Bloomsbury House, 74–77
Great Russell Street, London WC1B 3DA
Text © Philip Ardagh, 2020
Illustrations © Jason Chapman, 2020
Designed by Faber and Faber
ISBN 978–0–571–33117–8
Printed in India
10 9 8 7 6 5 4 3 2 1
The moral rights of Philip Ardagh
and Jason Chapman have been asserted.
A CIP record for this book is available
from the British Library.

# What's in the Truck?

Written by
**PHILIP ARDAGH**

Illustrated by
**JASON CHAPMAN**

faber

In **SCREECHES** Prince Ollie in a truck with **GIANT** wheels.

The back door flips open
and out something squeals...

a turbo-charged engine,
and gleaming chrome pipes.

It **ZOOMS** down the road, leaving tyre marks of black,

as it burns off the rubber...

**LooK!**

What's that
at the back?

Out glides a limo, as sleek as a plane,

with big, gleaming hubcaps
as bright as champagne.

It **purrrrrrs** down the road like a pedigree cat.

Swerves round a veg van.

Look out!

What a lucky escape,
      for the drivers at least!

And the pigs look so happy
with their vegetable feast.

It's an open-topped **sports car**, *perfect* for two.

It **SPEEDS** along nicely, and zips out of view.

The rider in helmet, goggles and leathers

**roars**
up to the palace
surrounded by heathers.

From the bike springs a scooter
that splashes through mud.

Ding-a-ling!
goes the doorbell.
Out steps a princess,

PULL

with diamond tiara
and best birthday dress...

Inside is a **Key**.

She hops in delight!
She laughs and she squeals
as she fires up the engine of...